ALLIGATOR WEDDING

Nancy Jewell

illustrated by
J. Rutland

Henry Holt and Company ✦ New York

Henry Holt and Company, LLC
Publishers since 1866
175 Fifth Avenue
New York, New York 10010
www.HenryHoltKids.com

Library of Congress Cataloging-in-Publication Data
Jewell, Nancy.
Alligator wedding / by Nancy Jewell ; illustrated by J. Rutland. — 1st ed.
p.   cm.
Summary: At the wedding of two alligators, held in the marshy glades of a bayou,
guests slither and slide under a swampland moon.
ISBN 978-0-8050-6819-1
[1. Stories in rhyme. 2. Alligators—Fiction. 3. Weddings—Fiction. 4. Bayous—Fiction.]
I. Rutland, J., ill. II. Title.
PZ8.3.J47Al 2010   [E]—dc22   2009005263

First Edition—2010 / Designed by Patrick Collins
The artist used acrylic paint on illustration board to create the art for this book.
Printed in January 2010 in China by South China Printing Company Ltd.,
Dongguan City, Guangdong Province, on acid-free paper. ∞

1 3 5 7 9 10 8 6 4 2

For Peggy Naderman
—N. J.

For Mom, Dad, Jeremy,
and my whole family
—J. R.

Down in the bayou
in the marshy glades
where the alligators slither and slide,
on a warm summer night
when the moon was bright,
an alligator took a bride.

In her gown of moss and her cobweb veil,
the bride made the groom's heart sing

as he slid over a claw
of her scaly green paw
a huge rock wedding ring.

Then he planted a kiss,
a big slurpy kiss,
on the bride's long, bumpy snout,
and the marshy reeds quivered
and the cypress trees shivered
with the guests' hurrahs and shouts.

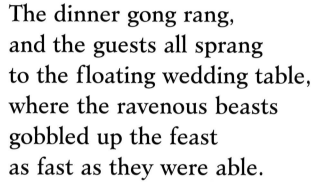

The dinner gong rang,
and the guests all sprang
to the floating wedding table,
where the ravenous beasts
gobbled up the feast
as fast as they were able.

Stuffed with Creole crab cakes,
gator gumbo stew, and Bayou breads,

they gulped swamp ade,
and, with snouts upraised,
belched toasts to the newlyweds.

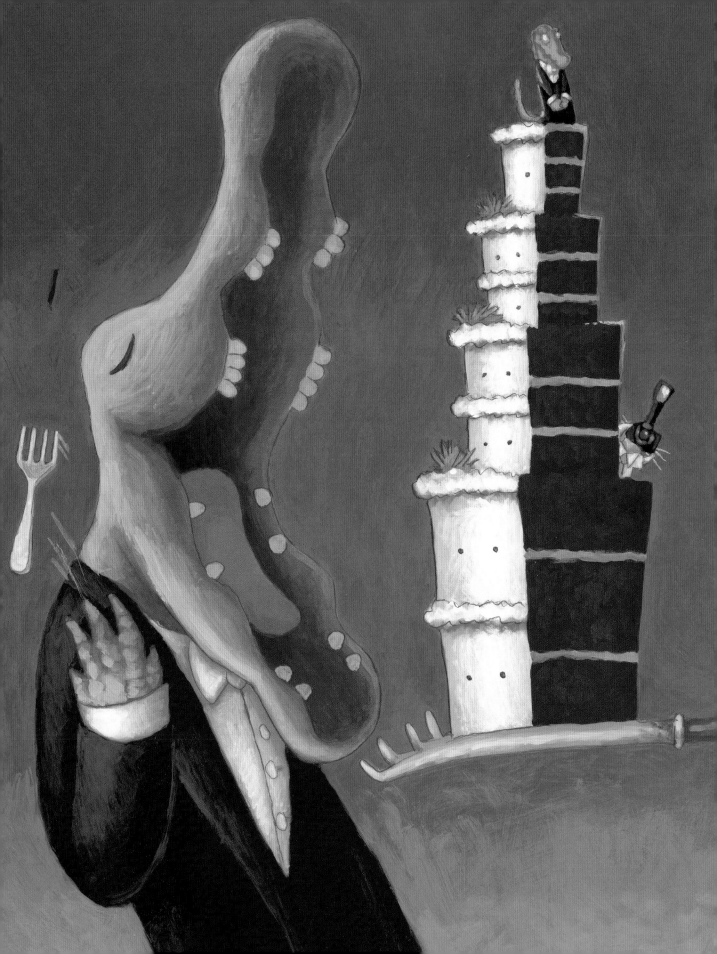

"Now," said the bride,
"it is time for dessert."
And she sliced off half the cake,
which she fed to the groom
for him to consume
on the end of a long-handled rake.

When the feasting was done,
the gator on the drum
began to tap out a tune,
and the guests began swaying,
swinging, and sashaying
beneath the swampland moon.

Then they all began to rock and roll
in the steamy, shimmering heat,

while the saxophone sobbed,
and the bass fiddle throbbed
to a frenzied bayou beat.

They did the Big Beast Boogie,

the Reptile Romp,

the Gumbo Gator Gallop,

and the Swampland Stomp.

Up and down the bayou
you could hear the sound
of those rowdy reptiles
pounding the ground.

Then it was time
for the hefty green bride
to toss her crawfish bouquet,
but she heaved it so high
in the swampland sky
that a pelican swept it away.

The honeymoon barge
was now drawing near,
towed by water rats,
and the guests all cheered
when the newlyweds appeared
in their elegant traveling hats.

When the muscular beauty
took a seat on the raft,
it almost sank from her weight,
and they needed a barge
to be twice as large
to support her heavier mate.

"Oh, no!" cried the groom.
"What *will* we do now?"
But the bride just smiled at him.

"Cheer up, my dear.
The solution is clear.
We'll get in the water and swim."

The beasts on shore
threw spicy rice
at the dear departing lovers,

and when the two
had swum from view,
they pelted one another.

Then those boisterous beasties
partied the night away,
collapsing asleep
in a snoring heap
at sunrise the next day.